The Yellow Star

The Legend of King Christian X of Denmark

To Queen Margrethe II of Denmark

—H. S.

To Ruby, Sam, Grace, Brady, and Jade

Ω

Published by
PEACHTREE PUBLISHING COMPANY INC.
1700 Chattahoochee Avenue
Atlanta, GA 30318-2112
PeachtreeBooks.com

First trade paperback published in 2020

Book design by Adela Pons

The illustrations were created in oil.

Manufactured in March 2022 by Leo Paper in China
30 29 28 27 26 25 24 23 (hardcover)
10 9 8 7 6 5 4 3 2 (trade paperback)

HC ISBN: 978-1-56145-208-8
PB ISBN: 978-1-68263-189-8

Library of Congress Cataloging-in-Publication Data

Deedy, Carmen Agra.
The yellow star : the legend of King Christian X of Denmark / Carmen Agra Deedy ; illustrated by Henri Sørensen.—1st edition.
p.cm.
Summary: Retells the story of King Christian X and the Danish resistance to the Nazis during World War II.
ISBN 1-56145-208-4
1. Christian X, King of Denmark, 1870–1947—Juvenile fiction. [1. Christian X, King of Denmark, 1870–1947—Fiction. 2. Denmark—History—German occupation, 1940–1945—Fiction.] I. Sørensen, Henri, ill. II. Title.
PZ7.D3587 Yg 2000
[Fic]—dc21   00-020602

The Yellow Star

The Legend of King Christian X of Denmark

Written by
Carmen Agra Deedy

Illustrated by
Henri Sørensen

PEACHTREE

ATLANTA

Early in the year 1940, in the country of Denmark, there were only Danes.

Tall Danes.

Stout Danes.

Old Danes.

Silly Danes.

Cranky Danes.

...and even some Great Danes.

But no matter how different from each other they seemed, the Danes held one thing in common: all were loyal subjects of their beloved King Christian.

Every morning, their king rode alone and unarmed along the streets of Denmark's capital, Copenhagen.

"Who's that?" a curious visitor once asked.

"Why, that's our King Christian!" his Danish host responded.

"Without a bodyguard?" asked the astonished guest.

"My friend," came the proud reply, "a king so loved needs no bodyguard. We Danes would all stand together in defense of our king."

Little did the Danes know how much they would need their wise king in the dark days to come.

Like a fierce storm, war was spreading across Europe, and even good King Christian was powerless to stop it.

Soon Nazi soldiers gathered like dark clouds at the Danish border. Their arrival in Copenhagen brought food shortages, curfews, and a new flag, which was hung at the palace.

The flag stood for war and fear and hatred.

The Danes watched and waited to see what their king would do.

King Christian sent a Danish soldier to remove the flag.

U pon discovering it missing, a Nazi officer demanded to see the king and asked, "Who took down the flag?"

"I sent a soldier to remove it," replied the king.

"Oh, you did, did you? Well, tomorrow another will fly in its place," the officer boasted.

"Then tomorrow I will send another soldier to remove it," countered the king.

"And I will have that man shot," threatened the Nazi.

Leaning forward, King Christian said evenly, "Then be prepared to shoot the king—for I will be that soldier."

The Nazi flag did not fly from the palace again.

The missing flag became a powerful symbol of resistance, and King Christian's subjects found reasons to pass the palace gates to see where it once hung.

Yet it was only a small victory; the king and his people's greatest test was still to come.

The terrible news arrived quietly, with leaflets that fluttered down on the city of Copenhagen:

Effective Immediately!

All Jews must sew onto their clothing a **YELLOW STAR** which must be visible **AT ALL TIMES!**

The people of Denmark were frightened. They had heard terrible stories. In some places, once Jews wore the yellow star, they were taken away and not heard from again.

As before, the people looked to their king.

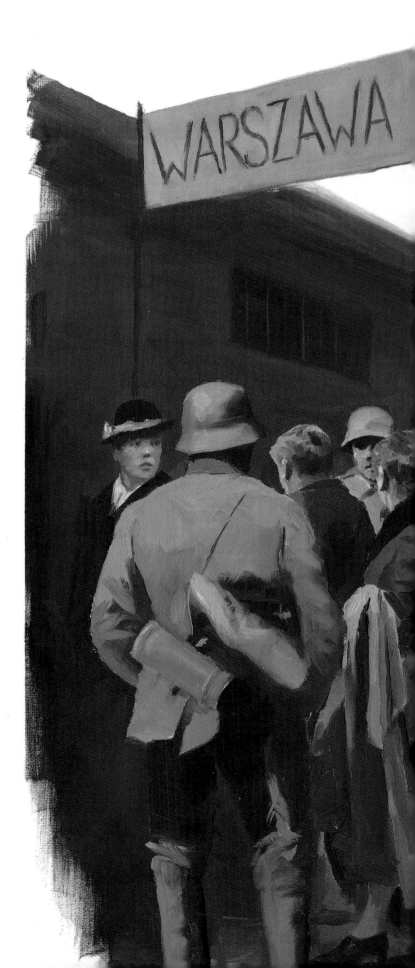

This time their king was as frightened as his people.

Without the yellow star to point them out, the Jews looked like any other Danes. Gentiles and Jews were all Danish subjects who worshiped God in different ways.

If King Christian called on the tiny Danish army to fight, Danes would die. If he did nothing, Danes would die.

Perhaps it was this riddle of the yellow star that drew King Christian to his balcony that night. The sky was filled with the light of many stars.

"If you wished to hide a star," wondered the king to himself, "where would you place it?" His eyes searched the heavens.

"Of course!" he thought. The answer was so simple. "You would hide it among its sisters."

The king summoned his tailor.

The tailor arrived and listened to the king's surprising request.

"We only have an hour before I ride at dawn," the king said urgently. "Can you complete this task in time?"

"Yes, your Highness. I'll begin immediately." The tailor bowed respectfully.

"And you do understand what this means?" the king insisted.

"I do, Your Highness, as will all your subjects," he answered with pride.

"I trust they will," whispered the king, placing as much faith in his Danish subjects as they had in him.

The following morning the King of Denmark, with courage and defiance, rode alone through Copenhagen. He was dressed in his finest clothing.

As they watched him pass, the subjects of King Christian understood what they should do.

And, once again, in the country of Denmark, there were only Danes.

Author's Note

The story of **The Yellow Star** is a legend. It may be disappointing to the reader, as it first was to this author, to learn there is no proof that the story ever occurred. I learned of it as a scrap of a tale told to me by a stranger. Its imagery was so compelling, and its humanity so palpable, that I wanted to know more. Over the years, despite collecting various oral versions of the story, researching documents and works of fiction (most notably Lois Lowry's moving novel, Number the Stars), I found only unauthenticated references to King Christian's legendary defiance.

And I learned of many facts that, in their own right, were as powerful as the legend itself. I learned that

- the beloved king of Denmark did indeed ride unescorted and unprotected through the streets of Copenhagen;
- stories about the king's support of Danish Jews began to circulate throughout Europe as early as 1943, including his threat to wear the yellow star in solidarity with the Jews;
- no Jews within Denmark were forced to wear the yellow star;

- among the Nazi-occupied countries, only Denmark rescued the overwhelming majority of its Jews;
- over 7,000 Danish Jews were smuggled to Sweden in fishing boats, 12 to 14 at a time, by a group of Danes called the "Helsingor Sewing Club;" and
- of the almost 500 Jews deported to Theresienstadt, all but 51 survived due in large part to the Danish government's intercession on their behalf.

Yet the legend only grows stronger. Why? Perhaps because we need it. The allegory of the yellow star used by the Nazis to divide and shame became in this legend a symbol of unity and hope. It is a story that should be told.

What if it had happened? What if every Dane, from shoemaker to priest, had worn the yellow Star of David?

And what if we could follow that example today against violations of human rights? What if the good and strong people of the world stood shoulder to shoulder, crowding the streets and filling the squares, saying, "You cannot do this injustice to our sisters and brothers, or you must do it to us as well."

What if?

—C. A. D.
2000

The author and publisher invite you to read in more detail about the Nazi occupation of Denmark during World War II and the Danish resistance movement. (For links to important sources on the subject, visit the Peachtree Publishing Company Inc. website at *www.peachtree-online.com/yellowstar*)